THE HOLES
Around Mars

I0534021

THE HOLES
Around Mars

JEROME BIXBY

ÆGYPAN PRESS

This story first in the January 1954 issue of *Galaxy Science Fiction.*

Special thanks to Greg Weeks and the Online Distributed Proofreading Team at http://www.pgdp.net.

The Holes Around Mars
A publication of
ÆGYPAN PRESS
www.aegypan.com

Science said it could not be, but there it was.
And whoosh — look out — here it is again!

*S*paceship crews should be selected on the basis of their non-irritating qualities as individuals. No chronic complainers, no hypochondriacs, no bugs on cleanliness — particularly no one-man parties. I speak from bitter experience.

Because on the first expedition to Mars, Hugh Allenby damned near drove us nuts with his puns. We finally got so we just ignored them.

But no one can ignore that classic last one — it's written right into the annals of astronomy, and it's there to stay.

Allenby, in command of the expedition, was first to set foot outside the ship. As he stepped down from the airlock of the *Mars I,* he placed that foot on a convenient rock, caught the toe of his weighted boot in a hole in the rock, wrenched his ankle and smote the ground with his pants.

Sitting there, eyes pained behind the transparent shield of his oxygen-mask, he stared at the rock.

*I*t was about five feet high. Ordinary granite — no special shape — and several inches below its summit, running straight through it in a northeasterly direction, was a neat round four-inch hole.

"I'm *upset* by the *hole* thing," he grunted.

The rest of us scrambled out of the ship and gathered around his plump form. Only one or two of us winced at his miserable double pun.

"Break anything, Hugh?" asked Burton, our pilot, kneeling beside him.

"Get out of my way, Burton," said Allenby. "You're obstructing my view."

Burton blinked. A man constructed of long bones and caution, he angled out of the way, looking around to see what he was obstructing view *of*.

He saw the rock and the round hole through it. He stood very still, staring. So did the rest of us.

"Well, I'll be damned," said Janus, our photographer. "A hole."

"In a rock," added Gonzales, our botanist.

"Round," said Randolph, our biologist.

"An *artifact*," finished Allenby softly.

Burton helped him to his feet. Silently we gathered around the rock.

Janus bent down and put an eye to one end of the hole. I bent down and looked through the other end. We squinted at each other.

As mineralogist, I was expected to opinionate. "Not drilled," I said slowly. "Not chipped. Not melted. Certainly not eroded."

I heard a rasping sound by my ear and straightened. Burton was scratching a thumbnail along the rim of the hole. "Weathered," he said. "Plenty old. But I'll bet it's a perfect circle, if we measure."

Janus was already fiddling with his camera, testing the cooperation of the tiny distant sun with a light-meter.

"Let us see *weather* it is or not," Allenby said.

Burton brought out a steel tape-measure. The hole was four and three-eighths inches across. It was perfectly circular and about sixteen inches long. And four feet above the ground.

"But why?" said Randolph. "Why should anyone bore a four-inch tunnel through a rock way out in the middle of the desert?"

"Religious symbol," said Janus. He looked around, one hand on his gun. "We'd better keep an eye out — maybe we've landed on sacred ground or something."

"A totem *hole*, perhaps," Allenby suggested.

"Oh. I don't know," Randolph said — to Janus, not Allenby. As I've mentioned, we always ignored Allenby's puns. "Note the lack of ornamentation. Not at all typical of religious articles."

"On Earth," Gonzales reminded him. "Besides, it might be utilitarian, not symbolic."

"Utilitarian, how?" asked Janus.

"An altar for snakes," Burton said dryly.

"Well," said Allenby, "you can't deny that it has its *holy* aspects."

"Get your hand away, will you, Peters?" asked Janus.

I did. When Janus's camera had clicked, I bent again and peered through the hole. "It sights on that low ridge over there," I said. "Maybe it's some kind of surveying setup. I'm going to take a look."

"Careful," warned Janus. "Remember, it may be sacred."

As I walked away, I heard Allenby say, "Take some scrapings from the inside of the hole, Gonzales. We might be able to determine if anything is kept in it. . . ."

One of the stumpy, purplish, barrel-type cacti on the ridge had a long vertical bite out of it . . . as if someone had carefully carved out a narrow U-shaped section from the top down, finishing the bottom of the U in a neat semicircle. It was as flat and cleancut as the inside surface of a horseshoe magnet.

I hollered. The others came running. I pointed.

"Oh, my God!" said Allenby. "Another one."

The pulp of the cactus in and around the U-hole was dried and dead-looking.

Silently Burton used his tape-measure. The hole measured four and three-eighths inches across. It was eleven inches deep. The semicircular bottom was about a foot above the ground.

"This ridge," I said, "is about three feet higher than where we landed the ship. I bet the hole in the rock and the hole in this cactus are on the same level."

Gonzales said slowly, "This was not done all at once. It is a result of periodic attacks. Look here and here. These overlapping depressions along the outer edges of the hole —" he pointed — "on this side of the cactus. They are the signs of repeated impact. And the scallop effect on *this* side, where whatever made the hole emerged. There are juices still oozing — not at the point of impact, where the plant is desiccated, but below, where the shock was transmitted —"

A distant shout turned us around. Burton was at the rock, beside the ship. He was bending down, his eye to the far side of the mysterious hole.

He looked for another second, then straightened and came toward us at a lope.

"They line up," he said when he reached us. "The bottom of the hole in the cactus is right in the middle when you sight through the hole in the rock."

"As if somebody came around and whacked the cactus regularly," Janus said, looking around warily.

[Illustration]

"To keep the line of sight through the holes clear?" I wondered. "Why not just remove the cactus?"

"Religious," Janus explained.

The gauntlet he had discarded lay ignored on the ground, in the shadow of the cactus. We went on past the ridge toward an outcropping of rock about a hundred yards farther on. We walked silently, each of us wondering if what we half-expected would really be there.

It was. In one of the tall, weathered spires in the outcropping, some ten feet below its peak and four feet above the ground, was a round four-inch hole.

Allenby sat down on a rock, nursing his ankle, and remarked that anybody who believed this crazy business was really happening must have holes in the rocks in his head.

[Illustration]

Burton put his eye to the hole and whistled. "Sixty feet long if it's an inch," he said. "The other end's just a pinpoint. But you can see it. The damn thing's perfectly straight."

I looked back the way we had come. The cactus stood on the ridge, with its U-shaped bite, and beyond was the ship, and beside it the perforated rock.

"If we surveyed," I said, "I bet the holes would all line up right to the last millimeter."

"But," Randolph complained, "why would anybody go out and bore holes in things all along a line through the desert?"

"Religious," Janus muttered. "It doesn't *have* to make sense."

*W*e stood there by the outcropping and looked out along the wide, red desert beyond. It stretched flatly for miles from this point, south toward Mars' equator — dead sandy wastes, crisscrossed by the "canals," which we had observed while landing to be great straggly patches of vegetation, probably strung along underground waterflows.

BLONG-G-G- . . . *st-st-st-* . . .

We jumped half out of our skins. Ozone bit at our nostrils. Our hair stirred in the electrical uproar.

"L-look," Janus chattered, lowering his smoking gun.

About forty feet to our left, a small rabbity creature poked its head from behind a rock and stared at us in utter horror.

Janus raised his gun again.

"Don't bother," said Allenby tiredly. "I don't think it intends to attack."

"But —"

"I'm sure it isn't a Martian with religious convictions."

Janus wet his lips and looked a little shamefaced. "I guess I'm kind of taut."

"That's what I *taut*," said Allenby.

The creature darted from behind its rock and, looking at us over its shoulder, employed six legs to make small but very fast tracks.

We turned our attention again to the desert. Far out, black against Mars' azure horizon, was a line of low hills.

"Shall we go look?" asked Burton, eyes gleaming at the mystery.

Janus hefted his gun nervously. It was still crackling faintly from the discharge. "I say let's get back to the ship!"

Allenby sighed. "My leg hurts." He studied the hills. "Give me the field-glasses."

Randolph handed them over. Allenby put them to the shield of his mask and adjusted them.

After a moment he sighed again. "There's a hole. On a plane surface that catches the Sun. A lousy damned round little impossible hole."

"Those hills," Burton observed, "must be thousands of feet thick."

*T*he argument lasted all the way back to the ship.

Janus, holding out for his belief that the whole thing was of religious origin, kept looking around for Martians as if he expected them to pour screaming from the hills.

Burton came up with the suggestion that perhaps the holes had been made by a disintegrator-ray.

"It's possible," Allenby admitted. "This might have been the scene of some great battle —"

"With only one such weapon?" I objected.

Allenby swore as he stumbled. "What do you mean?"

"I haven't seen any other lines of holes — only the one. In a battle, the whole joint should be cut up.

That was good for a few moments' silent thought. Then Allenby said, "It might have been brought out by one side as a last resort. Sort of an ace in the hole."

I resisted the temptation to mutiny. "But would even one such weapon, in battle make only *one* line of holes? Wouldn't it be played in an arc against the enemy? You know it would."

"Well —"

"Wouldn't it cut slices out of the landscape, instead of boring holes? And wouldn't it sway or vibrate enough to make the holes miles away from it something less than perfect circles?"

"It could have been very firmly mounted."

"Hugh, does that sound like a practical weapon to you?"

Two seconds of silence. "On the other hand," he said, "instead of a war, the whole thing might have been designed to frighten some primitive race — or even some kind of beast — the *hole* out of here. A demonstration —"

"Religious," Janus grumbled, still looking around.

We walked on, passing the cactus on the low ridge.

"Interesting," said Gonzales. "The evidence that whatever causes the phenomenon has happened again and again. I'm afraid that the war theory —"

"Oh, my God!" gasped Burton.

We stared at him.

"The ship," he whispered. "It's right in line with the holes! If whatever made them is still in operation. . . ."

"Run!" yelled Allenby, and we ran like fiends.

*W*e got the ship into the air, out of line with the holes to what we fervently hoped was safety, and then we realized we were admitting our fear that the mysterious hole-maker might still be lurking around.

Well, the evidence was all for it, as Gonzales had reminded us — that cactus had been oozing.

We cruised at twenty thousand feet and thought it over.

Janus, whose only training was in photography, said, "Some kind of omnivorous animal? Or bird? Eats rocks and everything?"

"I will not totally discount the notion of such an animal," Randolph said. "But I will resist to the death the suggestion that it forages with geometric precision."

After a while, Allenby said, "Land, Burton. By that 'canal.' Lots of plant life — fauna, too. We'll do a little collecting."

Burton set us down feather-light at the very edge of the sprawling flat expanse of vegetation, commenting that the scene reminded him of his native Texas pear-flats.

We wandered in the chilly air, each of us except Burton pursuing his specialty. Randolph relentlessly stalked another of the rabbity creatures. Gonzales was carefully digging up plants and stowing them in jars. Janus was busy with his cameras, recording every aspect of Mars transferable to film. Allenby walked around, helping anybody who needed it. An astronomer, he'd done half his work on the way to Mars and would do the other half on the return trip. Burton lounged in the Sun, his back against a ship's fin, and played chess with Allenby, who was calling out his moves in a bull roar. I grubbed for rocks.

My search took me farther and farther away from the others — all I could find around the 'canal' was gravel, and I wanted to chip at some big stuff. I walked toward a long rise a half-mile or so away, beyond which rose an enticing array of house-sized boulders.

As I moved out of earshot, I heard Randolph snarl, "Burton, *will* you stop yelling, 'Kt to B-2 and check?'"

Every time you open your yap, this critter takes off on
me."

Then I saw the groove.

*I*t started right where the ground began to rise — a
thin, shallow, curve-bottomed groove in the dirt at my
feet, about half an inch across, running off straight
toward higher ground.

With my eyes glued to it, I walked. The ground slowly
rose. The groove deepened, widened — now it was about
three inches across, about one and a half deep.

I walked on, holding my breath. Four inches wide.
Two inches deep.

The ground rose some more. Four and three-eighths
inches wide. I didn't have to measure it — I *knew*.

Now, as the ground rose, the edges of the groove
began to curve inward over the groove. They touched.
No more groove.

The ground had risen, the groove had stayed level
and gone underground.

Except that now it wasn't a groove. It was a round
tunnel.

A hole.

A few paces farther on, I thumped the ground with
my heel where the hole ought to be. The dirt crumbled,
and there was the little dark tunnel, running straight
in both directions.

I walked on, the ground falling away gradually again.
The entire process was repeated in reverse. A hairline
appeared in the dirt — widened — became lips that drew
slowly apart to reveal the neat straight four-inch groove
— which shrank as slowly to a shallow line of the
ground — and vanished.

I looked ahead of me. There was one low ridge of ground between me and the enormous boulders. A neat four-inch semicircle was bitten out of the very top of the ridge. In the house-sized boulder directly beyond was a four-inch hole.

*A*llenby winced and called the others when I came back and reported.

"The mystery *deepens,*" he told them. He turned to me. "Lead on, Peters. You're temporary *drill* leader."

Thank God he didn't say *Fall in.*

The holes went straight through the nest of boulders — there'd be a hole in one and, ten or twenty feet farther on in the next boulder, another hole. And then another, and another — right through the nest in a line. About thirty holes in all.

Burton, standing by the boulder I'd first seen, flashed his flashlight into the hole. Randolph, clear on the other side of the jumbled nest, eye to hole, saw it.

Straight as a string!

The ground sloped away on the far side of the nest — no holes were visible in that direction — just miles of desert. So, after we'd stared at the holes for a while and they didn't go away, we headed back for the canal.

"Is there any possibility," asked Janus, as we walked, "that it could be a natural phenomenon?"

"There are no straight lines in nature," Randolph said, a little shortly. "That goes for a bunch of circles in a straight line. And for perfect circles, too."

"A planet is a circle," objected Janus.

"An oblate spheroid," Allenby corrected.

"A planet's orbit —"

"An ellipse."

Janus walked a few steps, frowning. Then he said, "I remember reading that there *is* something darned near a perfect circle in nature." He paused a moment. "Potholes." And he looked at me, as mineralogist, to corroborate.

"What kind of potholes?" I asked cautiously. "Do you mean where part of a limestone deposit has dissol —"

"No. I once read that when a glacier passes over a hard rock that's lying on some softer rock, it grinds the hard rock down into the softer, and both of them sort of wear down to fit together, and it all ends up with a round hole in the soft rock."

"Probably neither stone," I told Janus, "would be homogenous. The softer parts would abrade faster in the soft stone. The end result wouldn't be a perfect circle."

Janus's face fell.

"Now," I said, "would anyone care to define this term 'perfect circle' we're throwing around so blithely? Because such holes as Janus describes are often pretty damned round."

Randolph said, "Well. . . ."

"It is settled, then," Gonzales said, a little sarcastically. "Your discussion, gentlemen, has established that the long, horizontal holes we have found were caused by glacial action."

"Oh, no," Janus argued seriously. "I once read that Mars never had any glaciers."

All of us shuddered.

*H*alf an hour later, we spotted more holes, about a mile down the 'canal,' still on a line, marching along the desert, through cacti, rocks, hills, even through one edge of the low vegetation of the 'canal' for thirty feet or so. It was the damnedest thing to bend down and look straight through all that curling, twisting growth . . . a round tunnel from either end.

We followed the holes for about a mile, to the rim of an enormous saucerlike valley that sank gradually before us until, miles away, it was thousands of feet deep. We stared out across it, wondering about the other side.

Allenby said determinedly, "We'll burrow to the *bottom* of these holes, once and for all. Back to the ship, men!"

We hiked back, climbed in and took off.

At an altitude of fifty feet, Burton lined the nose of the ship on the most recent line of holes and we flew out over the valley.

On the other side was a range of hefty hills. The holes went through them. Straight through. We would approach one hill — Burton would manipulate the front viewscreen until we spotted the hole — we would pass over the hill and spot the other end of the hole in the rear screen.

One hole was two hundred and eighty miles long.

Four hours later, we were halfway around Mars.

Randolph was sitting by a side port, chin on one hand, his eyes unbelieving. "All around the planet," he kept repeating. "All around the planet. . . ."

"Halfway at least," Allenby mused. "And we can assume that it continues in a straight line, through anything and everything that gets in its way. . . ." He gazed out the front port at the uneven blue-green haze of a 'canal' off to our left. "For the love of Heaven, why?"

Then Allenby fell down. We all did.

Burton had suddenly slapped at the control board, and the ship braked and sank like a plugged duck. At the last second, Burton propped up the nose with a short burst, the ten-foot wheels hit desert sand and in five hundred yards we had jounced to a stop.

Allenby got up from the floor. "Why did you do that?" he asked Burton politely, nursing a bruised elbow.

Burton's nose was almost touching the front port. "Look!" he said, and pointed.

About two miles away, the Martian village looked like a handful of yellow marbles flung on the desert.

*W*e checked our guns. We put on our oxygen-masks. We checked our guns again. We got out of the ship and made damned sure the airlock was locked.

An hour later, we crawled inch by painstaking inch up a high sand dune and poked our heads over the top.

The Martians were runts — the tallest of them less than five feet tall — and skinny as a pencil. Dried-up and brown, they wore loincloths of woven fiber.

They stood among the dusty-looking inverted-bowl buildings of their village, and every one of them was looking straight up at us with unblinking brown eyes.

The six safeties of our six guns clicked off like a rattle of dice. The Martians stood there and gawped.

"Probably a highly developed sense of hearing in this thin atmosphere," Allenby murmured. "Heard us coming."

"They thought that landing of Burton's was an earthquake," Randolph grumbled sourly.

"Marsquake," corrected Janus. One look at the village's scrawny occupants seemed to have convinced him that his life was in no danger.

Holding the Martians covered, we examined the village from atop the thirty-foot dune.

The domelike buildings were constructed of something that looked like adobe. No windows — probably built with sandstorms in mind. The doors were about halfway up the sloping sides, and from each door a stone ramp wound down around the house to the ground — again with sandstorms in mind, no doubt, so drifting dunes wouldn't block the entrances.

The center of the village was a wide street, a long sandy area some thirty feet wide. On either side of it, the houses were scattered at random, as if each Martian had simply hunted for a comfortable place to sit and then built a house around it.

"Look," whispered Randolph.

One Martian had stepped from a group situated on the far side of the street from us. He started to cross the street, his round brown eyes on us, his small bare feet plodding sand, and we saw that in addition to a loincloth he wore jewelry — a hammered metal ring, a bracelet on one skinny ankle. The Sun caught a copperish gleam on his bald narrow head, and we saw a band of metal there, just above where his eyebrows should have been.

"The super-chief," Allenby murmured. "Oh, *shaman* me!"

As the bejeweled Martian approached the center of the street, he glanced briefly at the ground at his feet. Then he raised his head, stepped with dignity across the exact center of the street and came on toward us, passing the dusty-looking buildings of his realm and the dusty-looking groups of his subjects.

He reached the slope of the dune we lay on, paused — and raised small hands over his head, palms toward us.

"I think," Allenby said, "that an anthropologist would give odds on that gesture meaning peace."

He stood up, holstered his gun — without buttoning the flap — and raised his own hands over his head. We all did.

*T*he Martian language consisted of squeaks.

We made friendly noises, the chief squeaked and pretty soon we were the center of a group of wide-eyed Martians, none of whom made a sound. Evidently no one dared peep while the chief spoke — very likely the most articulate Martians simply squeaked themselves into the job. Allenby, of course, said they just *squeaked by.*

He was going through the business of drawing concentric circles in the sand, pointing at the third orbit away from the Sun and thumping his chest. The crowd around us kept growing as more Martians emerged from the dome buildings to see what was going on. Down the winding ramps of the buildings on our side of the wide, sandy street they came — and from the buildings on the other side of the street, plodding through the sand, blinking brown eyes at us, not making a sound.

Allenby pointed at the third orbit and thumped his chest. The chief squeaked and thumped his own chest and pointed at the copperish band around his head. Then he pointed at Allenby.

"I seem to have conveyed to him," Allenby said dryly, "the fact that I'm chief of our party. Well, let's try again."

He started over on the orbits. He didn't seem to be getting anyplace, so the rest of us watched the Martians instead. A last handful was straggling across the wide street.

"Curious," said Gonzales. "Note what happens when they reach the center of the street."

Each Martian, upon reaching the center of the street, glanced at his feet — just for a moment — without even breaking stride. And then came on.

"What can they be looking at?" Gonzales wondered.

"The chief did it too," Burton mused. "Remember when he first came toward us?"

We all stared intently at the middle of the street. We saw absolutely nothing but sand.

The Martians milled around us and watched Allenby and his orbits. A Martian child appeared from between two buildings across the street. On six-inch legs, it started across, got halfway, glanced downward — and came on.

"I don't get it," Burton said. "What in hell are they *looking* at?"

The child reached the crowd and squeaked a thin, high note.

A number of things happened at once.

*S*everal members of the group around us glanced down, and along the edge of the crowd nearest the center of the street there was a mild stir as individuals drifted off to either side. Quite casually — nothing at all urgent about it. They just moved concertedly to get farther away from the center of the street, not taking their interested gaze off us for one second in the process.

Even the chief glanced up from Allenby's concentric circles at the child's squeak. And Randolph, who had been fidgeting uncomfortably and paying very little attention to our conversation, decided that he must answer Nature's call. He moved off into the dunes surrounding the village. Or rather, he started to move.

The moment he set off across the wide street, the little Martian chief was in front of him, brown eyes wide, hands out before him as if to thrust Randolph back.

Again six safeties clicked. The Martians didn't even blink at the sudden appearance of our guns. Probably the only weapon they recognized was a club, or maybe a rock.

"What can the matter be?" Randolph said.

He took another step forward. The chief squeaked and stood his ground. Randolph had to stop or bump into him. Randolph stopped.

The chief squeaked, looking right into the bore of Randolph's gun.

"Hold still," Allenby told Randolph, "till we know what's up."

Allenby made an interrogative sound at the chief. The chief squeaked and pointed at the ground. We looked. He was pointing at his shadow.

Randolph stirred uncomfortably.

"Hold still," Allenby warned him, and again he made the questioning sound.

The chief pointed up the street. Then he pointed down the street. He bent to touch his shadow, thumping it with thin fingers. Then he pointed at the wall of a house nearby.

We all looked.

Straight lines had been painted on the curved brick-colored wall, up and down and across, to form many small squares about four inches across. In each square was a bit of squiggly writing, in blackish paint, and a small wooden peg jutting out from the wall.

Burton said, "Looks like a damn crossword puzzle."

"Look," said Janus. "In the lower right corner — a metal ring hanging from one of the pegs."

*A*nd that was all we saw on the wall. Hundreds of squares with figures in them — a small peg set in each — and a ring hanging on one of the pegs.

"You know what?" Allenby said slowly. "I think it's a calendar! Just a second — thirty squares wide by twenty-two high — that's six hundred and sixty. And that bottom line has twenty-six — twenty-*seven* squares. Six hundred and eighty-seven squares in all. That's how many days there are in the Martian year!"

He looked thoughtfully at the metal ring. "I'll bet that ring is hanging from the peg in the square that represents *today*. They must move it along every day, to keep track. . . ."

"What's a calendar got to do with my crossing the street?" Randolph asked in a pained tone.

He started to take another step. The chief squeaked as if it were a matter of desperate concern that he make us understand. Randolph stopped again and swore impatiently.

Allenby made his questioning sound again.

The chief pointed emphatically at his shadow, then at the communal calendar — and we could see now that he was pointing at the metal ring.

Burton said slowly, "I think he's trying to tell us that this is *today*. And such-and-such a *time* of day. I bet he's using his shadow as a sundial."

"Perhaps," Allenby granted.

Randolph said, "If this monkey doesn't let me go in another minute —"

The chief squeaked, eyes concerned.

"Stand still," Allenby ordered. "He's trying to warn you of some danger."

The chief pointed down the street again and, instead of squealing, revealed that there was another sound at his command. He said, "Whooooooosh!"

We all stared at the end of the street.

Nothing! Just the wide avenue between the houses, and the high sand dune down at the end of it, from which we had first looked upon the village.

The chief described a large circle with one hand, sweeping the hand above his head, down to his knees, up again, as fast as he could. He pursed his monkey-lips and said, "Whooooooosh!" And made the circle again.

A Martian emerged from the door in the side of a house across the avenue and blinked at the Sun, as if he had just awakened. Then he saw what was going on below and blinked again, this time in interest. He made his way down around the winding lamp and started to cross the street.

About halfway, he paused, eyed the calendar on the house wall, glanced at his shadow. Then he got down on his hands and knees and *crawled* across the middle of the street. Once past the middle, he rose, walked the rest of the way to join one of the groups and calmly stared at us along with the rest of them.

"They're all crazy," Randolph said disgustedly. "I'm going to cross that street!"

"Shut up. So it's a certain time of a certain day," Allenby mused. "And from the way the chief is acting, he's afraid for you to cross the street. And that other one just *crawled*. By God, do you know what this might tie in with?"

We were silent for a moment. Then Gonzales said, "Of course!"

And Burton said, "The *holes!*"

"Exactly," said Allenby. "Maybe whatever made — or makes — the holes comes right down the center of the street here. Maybe that's why they built the village this way — to make room for —"

"For what?" Randolph asked unhappily, shifting his feet.

"I don't know," Allenby said. He looked thoughtfully at the chief. "That circular motion he made — could he have been describing something that went around and around the planet? Something like — oh, no!" Allenby's eyes glazed. "I wouldn't believe it in a million years."

His gaze went to the far end of the street, to the high sand dune that rose there. The chief seemed to be waiting for something to happen.

"I'm going to crawl," Randolph stated. He got to his hands and knees and began to creep across the center of the avenue.

The chief let him go.

The sand dune at the end of the street suddenly erupted. A forty-foot spout of dust shot straight out from the sloping side, as if a bullet had emerged. Powdered sand hazed the air, yellowed it almost the full length of the avenue. Grains of sand stung the skin and rattled minutely on the houses.

WhoooSSSHHHHH!

Randolph dropped flat on his belly. He didn't have to continue his trip. He had made other arrangements.

*T*hat night in the ship, while we all sat around, still shaking our heads every once in a while, Allenby talked with Earth. He sat there, wearing the headphones, trying to make himself understood above the godawful static.

"... an exceedingly small body," he repeated wearily to his unbelieving audience, "about four inches in diameter. It travels at a mean distance of four feet above the surface of the planet, at a velocity yet to be calculated. Its unique nature results in many hitherto unobserved — I might say even unimagined — phenomena." He stared blankly in front of him for a moment, then delivered the understatement of his life. "The discovery may necessitate a re-examination of many of our basic postulates in the physical sciences."

The headphones squawked.

Patiently, Allenby assured Earth that he was entirely serious, and reiterated the results of his observations. I suppose that he, an astronomer, was twice as flabbergasted as the rest of us. On the other hand, perhaps he was better equipped to adjust to the evidence.

"Evidently," he said, "when the body was formed, it traveled at such fantastic velocity as to enable it to —" his voice was almost a whisper — "to punch holes in things."

The headphones squawked.

"In rocks," Allenby said, "in mountains, in anything that got in its way. And now the holes form a large portion of its fixed orbit."

Squawk.

"Its mass must be on the order of —"

Squawk.

"— process of making the holes slowed it, so that now it travels just fast enough —"

Squawk.

"— maintain its orbit and penetrate occasional objects such as —"

Squawk.

"— and sand dunes —"

Squawk.

"My God, I *know* it's a mathematical monstrosity," Allenby snarled. *"I didn't put it there!"*

Squawk.

Allenby was silent for a moment. Then he said slowly, "A name?"

Squawk.

"H'm," said Allenby. "Well, well." He appeared to brighten just a little. "So it's up to me, as leader of the expedition, to name it?"

Squawk.

"Well, well," he said.

That chop-licking tone was in his voice. We'd heard it all too often before. We shuddered, waiting.

"Inasmuch as Mars' outermost moon is called Deimos, and the next Phobos," he said, "I think I shall name the third moon of Mars — *Bottomos.*"

— JEROME BIXBY

www.ingramcontent.com/pod-product-compliance
Lightning Source LLC
Chambersburg PA
CBHW031906170626
46807CB00004B/1915